Cover and book design: Diane Goldsmith
Cover photograph © Paul Berquist
Back cover photographs © Paul Berquist

Library of Congress Cataloging-in-Publication Data

Skramstad, Jill.
    Wildlife Southwest. / text by Jill Skramstad.
      p.   cm. – (Chronicle junior nature series)
     Summary: Profiles twenty-five animals that can be seen in the
southwestern United States, including coyote, bobcat, and pronghorn.
   ISBN 0-8118-0126-8
    1. Zoology–Southwest. New–Juvenile literature. [1. Zoology–
–Southwest. New.] I. Chronicle Books (Firm) II. Title.
III. Series.
QL 155.W56 1992
599.0979–dc20   91-30939
                                  CIP
                                  AC

Distributed in Canada by Raincoast Books, 112 East Third Avenue, Vancouver, B.C. V5T 1C8

10 9 8 7 6 5 4 3 2 1

Chronicle Books, 275 Fifth Street, San Francisco, California 94103

Acknowledgments

Chronicle Books would like to give special thanks to the following people from the national parks and monuments in the Southwest region for their ideas, suggestions, enthusiasm, and willingness to approve the text and contents of this book: John Ray, *Resource Management Specialist,* Grand Canyon National Park; Paul Feinberg, *Biological Technician,* Grand Canyon National Park; Jim Barnett, *Chief Naturalist,* Organ Pipe Cactus National Monument; Tom Denton, *Chief of Interpretation,* Saguaro National Monument; Terry Maze, *Chief of Interpretation,* Petrified Forest National Park; Sonya Paspal, *Ranger,* Arches National Park; Susan Colclazer, *Chief of Interpretation,* Bryce Canyon National Park; Linda Ryan, *Interpretative Division,* Bryce Canyon National Park; Robert Mack, *Naturalist,* Capitol Reef National Park; Tim Graham, *Resource Management,* Canyonlands National Park; Dennis Carruth, *Resource Management,* Carlsbad Caverns National Park; Terry Nichols, *Chief Naturalist,* Aztec Ruins National Monument; *Resource Management Division,* Mesa Verde National Park; Sue Fisher, *Ranger,* Great Sand Dunes National Monument.

And to the talented photographers who have contributed to this book:
Paul Berquist/Tuscon, AZ © pp. 4, 8, 16, 19, 20, 23, 24, 28, 31, 32, 35, 36, 44, 47, 48, 51, 52.
Buff Corsi © p. 15.
John Hendrickson © pp. 7, 11, 39, 40.
B. "Moose" Peterson/Wildlife Research Photography © pp. 27, 43.
Kennan Ward © p. 12.

WILDLIFE
SOUTHWEST

TEXT BY JILL SKRAMSTAD

Chronicle Junior Nature Series

CHRONICLE BOOKS • SAN FRANCISCO

CONTENTS

INTRODUCTION

People from all over the world are drawn to the American Southwest. It is a magical place of surprising colors and shapes. There are varying opinions about what areas are included in the Southwest. Most people, however, agree that Utah, Arizona, New Mexico, and Colorado make up the central part of the Southwest. This book covers some of the animals that can be found in these four states.

Much of the Southwest looks like desert, even though technically large parts of the area are not desert at all. The definition of a desert is complex. Just because an area is dry or empty looking does not necessarily make it a desert. Whether a certain area is desert or not is determined by the amount of rain or snow it gets, as well as by how much water evaporates. If more water evaporates than falls as rain or snow, then the area is a desert. This means that a desert can be hot or cold, rocky or sandy. You can explore four different deserts in the Southwest: the Great Basin, Sonoran, Chihuahuan, and the Colorado Plateau. Each has its own characteristics and climate and provides its own special habitats and challenges for wildlife.

The lack of water and the harsh climate of the Southwest makes it difficult for animals to survive, but many species have found ingenious ways of living here. In fact, the Southwest is home to a great variety of animals. Many of the animals living in the Southwest, like the coyote and the mule deer, may already be familiar to you because they are also found in other areas of the country. Some, like the horny toad with its thick, dry skin, have developed special body parts. And others like the desert tortoise are rare and need our help if they are to continue to exist.

As you look for wildlife, you can enjoy learning how each animal has made adjustments to live in a desert environment. Even if you don't see any wildlife at all you can always listen for them or look for their tracks and signs. The national parks and monuments of the Southwest are excellent places to look for wildlife. We hope this guide will help you learn about the diversity of animals found throughout this region, while at the same time help you develop a lasting appreciation and respect for our fragile environment.

— Ellis Richard *Park Naturalist*
Grand Canyon National Park

TRACKING THE SOUTHWEST'S WILDLIFE PRESERVES

ARIZONA PARKS
1 Grand Canyon National Park
2 Petrified Forest National Park
3 Canyon de Chelly National Monument
4 Organ Pipe Cactus National Monument
5 Saguaro National Monument

COLORADO PARKS
6 Mesa Verde National Park
7 Black Canyon of the Gunnison National Monument
8 Dinosaur National Monument
9 Great Sand Dunes National Monument
10 Curecanti National Recreation Area

NEW MEXICO PARKS
11 Carlsbad Caverns National Park
12 Aztec Ruins National Monument
13 Gila Cliff Dwellings National Monument
14 Pecos National Monument
15 White Sands National Monument

UTAH PARKS
16 Arches National Park
17 Bryce Canyon National Park
18 Canyonlands National Park
19 Capitol Reef National Park
20 Zion National Park

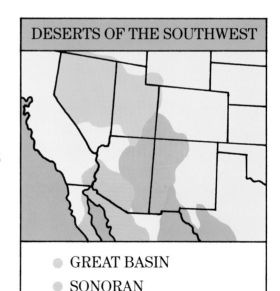

DESERTS OF THE SOUTHWEST

- GREAT BASIN
- SONORAN
- CHIHUAHUAN
- COLORADO PLATEAU

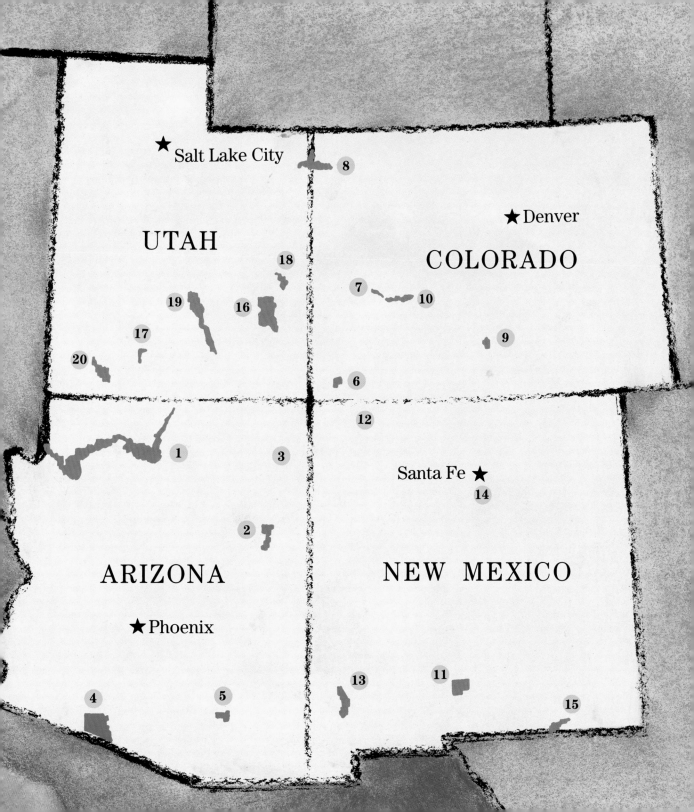

Mule deer are a species of deer named for their big ears, which resemble those of a mule. When its ears are erect and forward, the deer is alert and listening carefully. When its ears are laid back, it is frightened and trying to hide.

M ule deer are one of the most common desert mammals and can be found in all regions of the Southwest—in the lower desert, where they live in low brush and cacti, and in the higher desert, where tall trees provide shelter. They can also be seen in meadows, around campgrounds, and in open areas along roadsides. Mule deer are three to four feet tall and can weigh as much as two hundred pounds. Their diet consists mainly of grass, twigs, and cactus fruits.

The male deer, or buck, can be easily identified by his large forked antlers. These antlers are shed every winter, and new ones

MULE DEER

are regrown in the summer. While they are developing, the antlers are covered with a soft, velvety skin that dries, loosens, and eventually falls off or gets rubbed away by the deer. Bucks use their antlers both to protect themselves and to compete with other bucks for mates. The mating season of the mule deer occurs in the fall, and in late May or early June the female deer, or doe, gives birth to one or two spotted fawns. Newborn fawns cannot walk very well and spend much of their time curled up on the ground. Their white-spotted coat acts as camouflage, blending into the coloration of the ground and concealing the young deer from its enemies. The spots disappear after two to three months, and the fawns stay with their mothers until they are about a year old.

The main predator of the mule deer is the mountain lion, although bobcats and coyotes sometimes hunt the deer for food as well. The mule deer is very fast. It can reach speeds of thirty-five miles an hour and jump as far as twenty-five feet. This quickness, along with strong hooves that can be used as weapons, helps protect the mule deer from its enemies.

The pronghorn is the fastest land mammal in North America and the second fastest in the world, surpassed only by the African cheetah. Adult pronghorns are capable of reaching speeds of forty-five miles per hour and leaping twenty-five feet or more, which makes it easy for them to outdistance their most dangerous predators, the coyote and the wolf. Whereas members of the deer family, like the mule deer, have antlers, pronghorns have horns. Antlers are generally branched, are covered with a soft coating that falls off as it dries, and are shed each year. Horns, on the other hand, are bony cores covered with a hard sheath and, except for the pronghorn, are not branched or shed.

PRONGHORN

Pronghorns are herbivorous and prefer to live in shrub or grassland habitats where they can easily find sagebrush, rabbitbrush, and grass to eat. They are three feet tall and weigh up to one hundred and twenty-five pounds. Bucks fight for a mate in the late summer, and a single buck will gather as many as fifteen does in a harem. In May or June, when the doe is ready to give birth, she leaves the harem seeking solitude. Females give birth to one to three, and usually two, fawns. The fawn weighs eight pounds at birth and can outrun a human by the time it is four days old.

Once great herds of pronghorns ranged across the midwestern plains, reaching all the way to the Pacific Ocean. In the 1920s the number of pronghorns reached a record low of only thirteen thousand because hunting, railroads, competition for food with livestock, and other human developments forced the pronghorns out of their home range. Today their numbers are slowly increasing as small, scattered herds appear throughout the Southwest. The pronghorn's comeback has been greatly helped by the setting aside of wildlife preserves such as our national parks and monuments.

The cinnamon-colored pronghorn has a distinctive black mask on its face, long pointed ears, a white belly and rump, and shiny black horns. Although both males and females grow horns, the males' have one or two distinctive prongs that give the animal its name.

Bobcats are most active at night, although they often prowl for food during the day as well. Animals that are active at night are nocturnal. The best place to look for bobcats is in steep canyon country or in rocky, thick-brushed areas at dusk and at night.

A member of the cat family, the bobcat is the smallest and most common of native wildcats still roaming the West. Although there are many bobcats throughout the Southwest, because of their shy, solitary nature few are ever seen. Like all members of the cat family, the bobcat is carnivorous. Rodents, rabbits, and hares make up most of the bobcat's diet, although it will occasionally eat pronghorns or ground-nesting birds.

Named for its short, stubby tail, the bobcat has a reddish brown coat that is sprinkled with black spots, pointed ears, long hair, and small feet. An adult weighs between fifteen and thirty-five pounds and measures thirty to thirty-six inches in length, counting its tail.

BOBCAT

The bobcat usually lives in an underground den that has been abandoned by some other animal but is also comfortable on a rocky ledge, a cliff face, or in a hollow log. In January or February the female cat is ready to mate, and during this time bobcats can be one of the noisiest animals in the desert. The bobcat's mating call is a loud, shrill scream that sounds much like an alley cat. After a seven- to ten-week growing, or gestation, period, one to four baby kittens are born. Soon after birth, the female chases the male from the den, and the father plays no part in raising the young.

Two of the bobcat's greatest assets are its keen hearing and excellent eyesight. Both of these characteristics help warn the bobcat when someone or something approaches so it can quietly sneak away before it's discovered. The bobcat has few natural predators. Humans present the biggest threat because they often kill bobcats for their beautiful pelts, which are then made into fur coats.

The coyote is at home in almost any climate and in all types of terrain, perhaps making it the most well adapted and widespread mammal in the United States. A member of the dog family, a full-grown coyote is four feet long, including its tail, and weighs from twenty to fifty pounds. Coyotes have yellowish to brownish fur streaked with black, a black- or brown-tipped tail, and long pointed ears. Although active both day and night, the coyote is primarily nocturnal. Coyotes are most lively at dusk and dawn and can often be heard calling to each other with a series of short yips and howls.

COYOTE

The coyote is omnivorous, hunting for whatever it can find. Feeding primarily on snakes, rats, squirrels, and rabbits, a hungry coyote has been known to prey on larger animals like the pronghorn and mule deer; when food is really scarce, it will even eat cactus fruits. Coyotes usually hunt alone out in the open, and their hunting helps control the population of small rodents. The coyote lives in dens that are underground, in the roots of large trees, or in hills of dirt. These dens often have long tunnels with many connecting rooms.

The coyote stays with a single mate for years, sometimes for its entire life. Mating occurs in January and February, and five to ten pups are born in April or May. The pups weigh seven to ten ounces each and are raised by both parents until they are six months old. The adult coyote's main predator is the mountain lion. A young coyote, however, can easily fall into the hungry mouth of a bobcat or an eagle.

Desert coyotes are like other coyotes, but smaller and with lighter-colored fur. Once inhabiting only the western prairies, coyotes have now been recorded in almost every state and are especially common in the Southwest.

Like most other mammals that live in the hot, dry desert, the gray fox is nocturnal and spends most of its day underground in a den, resting in the shade, or napping on cool rocks.

A relative of the coyote, the fox is also a member of the dog family. Three common species of fox roam the Southwest deserts: red, gray, and kit. The gray and kit are the most common and can be seen throughout the Southwest, especially in canyons and rocky country. It is easy to tell the two apart by their size. The kit fox is the smallest of the foxes, weighing only three to six pounds, whereas the gray is the largest, weighing an average of ten to fifteen pounds and measuring forty-five inches long, including

GRAY FOX

its bushy tail. As its name suggests, the gray fox is gray with orange or reddish fur on its sides and throat. It has long ears, a black-tipped tail, and black patches on its muzzle.

The gray fox is the only species of fox that can climb trees, and in the higher desert elevations it will often rest above the ground in a hollow tree. Most of the time, however, gray foxes live and seek safety from eagles, coyotes, and bobcats in a deep underground burrow or under rocks. Gray foxes mate in the winter, and approximately fifty-three days later, a litter of three to seven babies is born. The baby foxes, called kits, weigh four ounces at birth and don't open their eyes for eleven days. The father moves out of the den when the kits are born but continues to bring his family food. Baby kits are raised by both parents and remain with them until autumn.

The gray fox is omnivorous, feeding on just about anything it can find, from kangaroo rats and jack rabbits to snakes, insects, birds, and even cactus fruits. Because the gray fox lacks the speed of the coyote, it must sneak up on its prey from behind. Often it will sit hunched for hours waiting for unsuspecting prey to cross its path. The gray fox then kills its prey by biting down with sharp teeth or with a powerful blow from its strong paws.

Badgers can dig a hole with their claws faster than a human can dig with a shovel. Because of this powerful burrowing ability, the badger is often mistaken for a rodent, but it is actually a member of the weasel family. The badger weighs from fifteen to thirty pounds, measures thirty inches in length, including its tail, and has short legs and small ears. Generally tan or gray with black feet, the badger is recognized by a white streak running down the middle of its face and head. Badgers live throughout the Southwest, especially in lower elevations and valleys.

BADGER

The badger digs a new place to sleep almost every night, so it is easy to discover where a badger lives—just look for patches of ground with many holes and tunnels. Badgers remain in a single den for longer time periods during the winter and when their young are small. Two to four furry babies are born in late spring or early summer. Their eyes open after six weeks, and they remain with their mother for several months.

The badger is primarily nocturnal. Although it is most active at night, badgers do hunt rodents in the mornings and late afternoons and sometimes even during the middle of the day. Using its sharp two-inch claws, the badger captures its prey by digging down into the burrow of a squirrel, a rat, or a prairie dog, capturing the animal in its home rather than waiting for the prey to come out. Badgers also eat insects, reptiles, and birds. Badgers avoid predators by retreating or tunneling underground. If they cannot escape, badgers will use their claws and razor-sharp teeth as weapons. If the enemy still does not retreat, the badger is also protected by its thick fur and tough skin.

Although badgers also live in grasslands and forests, they are well suited to desert life. Their sharp claws and long, flat bodies make it easy for them to bury themselves in piles of dirt to cool off or dig underneath rocks to build a home.

Ringtails are excellent climbers and use this skill to search for prey from high above ground on an exposed perch. Sometimes they can be seen hanging upside down by their hind feet and tail from a branch.

Ringtails look like a cross between a raccoon and a squirrel, but actually they make up a separate species within the raccoon family. Distinguished by the eight black rings on its tail, a ringtail can be identified by its large eyes, short legs, and long snout and tail. Ringtails weigh two pounds and measure up to thirty inches long, half of which is tail. The ringtail is common throughout the Southwest but is rarely seen because of its nocturnal nature. Found as far north as Utah, it lives in rocky canyon areas and in caves.

RINGTAIL

Although excellent hearing helps this mammal avoid human contact, it can occasionally be found foraging for food around campgrounds at night.

Ringtails, sometimes called the miner's cat or the ringed cat, display catlike characteristics such as licking themselves clean and constantly grooming their coats. Their nests are made out of bark, grass, leaves, or moss and are placed in a den hidden in bushes or twigs. In these nests three to four young are born in May or June after a gestation period of two months. Born blind and helpless, the babies weigh less than an ounce, about the same size as a newborn kitten. The male helps raise the young by bringing food to the kits and their nursing mother. After four weeks the kits' eyes open, and after eight weeks they leave the den.

Ringtails are carnivorous, and although they actually prefer to eat lizards, rats, and rabbits, they live primarily on insects, cactus fruits, and berries. The shy ringtail has few predators, though it is most often hunted by the great horned owl and the bobcat.

Twenty-two inches long and weighing four to five pounds, the black-tailed jack rabbit can be distinguished by its black ear tips, a black-streaked tail, and strong hind legs. Found in all areas of the Southwest, jack rabbits are most often sighted at dawn or dusk. The black-tailed jack rabbit has giant ears that can grow to be six inches long, making it one of the easiest animals to identify. The jack rabbit can listen in all directions at once because its ears can turn around in a complete circle. The jack rabbit's constantly twitching nose offers a tell-tale sign that it also has a keen sense of smell.

BLACK-TAILED JACK RABBIT

Although they are called jack rabbits, these mammals are actually hares, not rabbits. Hares are larger and have longer ears and legs than rabbits do. Baby rabbits, like the cottontail, are born blind and without much hair, whereas baby hares, like the jack rabbit, are born with their eyes open, fully haired, and ready to run within hours after birth. Jack rabbits make their nests in hollowed-out cacti or in clumps of grass and give birth to several litters a year, each consisting of three to six young. They are primarily nocturnal but often come out during the day to graze. Jack rabbits are herbivorous, eating grass, cactus fruits, and mesquite branches.

Capable of reaching speeds of up to thirty-five miles per hour in a matter of seconds, the swift jack rabbit makes huge leaps as it flees its pursuer. Every fourth or fifth leap is especially high so the hare can spot any predators over the brush. This quickness is essential to the jack rabbit's survival since it is one of the most hunted creatures in the desert. Its enemies include nearly all the carnivores, but primarily foxes, coyotes, bobcats, snakes, and birds of prey.

The jack rabbit's long ears are one of its most important features. These ears provide excellent long-distance hearing as well as the ability to maintain a constant body temperature by releasing excess heat.

As its name implies, the rock squirrel prefers rocky areas where its gray or brownish gray coloring easily blends with the rocks and boulders, camouflaging the squirrel from its enemies.

The rock squirrel is a member of the ground squirrel family. Twenty inches long, including its nine-inch bushy tail, it weighs just under two pounds and has short ears and white feet. The rock squirrel is common throughout the Southwest, from the high mountains to the desert floor, and can be discovered by listening for its high-pitched whistle.

Unlike most desert animals, ground squirrels are diurnal, which means that they are most active in the daytime. They live in open, dry areas feeding on cactus fruits, berries, bird eggs, nuts, seeds, and insects. Like a chipmunk, the ground squirrel stuffs food into its cheeks and then scampers off to store the food in its burrow. With

ROCK SQUIRREL

its sharp teeth and strong claws, the rock squirrel makes its burrow underground, beneath rocks, or between the roots of trees. During the summer, rock squirrels eat more than usual, and by fall a thick layer of fat has accumulated on their bodies. This extra weight helps keep the rock squirrel warm during the cold winter months when it is inactive. In many parts of the Southwest, however, rock squirrels are active all year. At higher elevations, rock squirrels hibernate for a few short weeks, and in hotter areas they may also rest during the warmest parts of the summer. This summer sleep is called estivation.

Rock squirrels are not social animals. Except for a mother with her young, it is unusual to see several together. During the early summer, five to seven young are born after a short gestation period of approximately four weeks. Raised solely by their mother, young rock squirrels mature quickly. Because of their small size, rock squirrels fall prey to many animals. Their chief predators include hawks, snakes, badgers, and coyotes.

Like rock squirrels and chipmunks, antelope squirrels are also members of the ground squirrel family. They are often confused with chipmunks because they are similar in both size and appearance, but antelope squirrels don't have stripes on their face. Three species of antelope squirrel inhabit the Southwest. The most widespread is the white-tailed, which lives in western Arizona, southeastern Utah, and northwestern New Mexico. Closely related is Harris' antelope squirrel, which lives primarily in southern Arizona, and the Texas antelope squirrel, which lives in New Mexico. All species of antelope squirrel have similar habits and appearances. Averaging nine inches in length, including its tail, antelope squirrels weigh approximately four and a half ounces.

ANTELOPE SQUIRREL

Antelope squirrels have a unique way of keeping cool in the desert heat. The squirrel washes its head with saliva from its mouth and is then cooled as the moisture evaporates. This survival technique allows the animal to be diurnal like its other ground squirrel relatives. Another means of keeping itself from overheating is the unusual way the squirrel travels across the desert. Running with its tail raised and flat against its back, the antelope squirrel is able to shade itself from the heat of the sun by reflecting the heat away with the white underside of its tail.

Like most other small mammals, antelope squirrels produce several litters a year. A litter of five to nine young is born in February or March, and another litter of the same size is generally born later in the year. Because of its small size, the antelope squirrel has many enemies. Two of its main predators include the badger and the rattlesnake.

The antelope squirrel gets most of its moisture from eating green plants, like cacti, and by drinking as much water as it can. Its diet also includes beetles, grasshoppers, and other insects.

Woodrats usually live alone in a nest lined with grass, sticks, and rocks. Pieces of prickly cactus are also used to keep other animals away. Woodrat homes may contain more than one nest and a number of entrances to provide easy escape from intruders.

Forty percent of all mammals are rodents, making rodents by far the largest order of mammals. Rodents include such animals as woodrats, beavers, porcupines, rats, gerbils, and hamsters; all have large, chisel-like teeth and a keen sense of hearing. Six species of woodrat live in the Southwest, and at least one species can be found in every park. The most common southwestern species are the white-throated, desert, Mexican, and bushy-tailed woodrats. All woodrats are similar in appearance, with gray or brownish coats, white bellies and feet, and a hairy tail.

WOODRAT

Woodrats are known for their marvelously constructed houses. High mounds of shredded bark, twigs, sticks, and pieces of cactus, these nests may be on the ground, in the crevice of a rock, or even in a tree. Also known as trade rats or packrats, woodrats will often drop whatever they are carrying and replace it with anything new that catches their eye. They have been known to snatch anything from keys to coins to cooking utensils. Despite their large numbers, woodrats are rarely seen because of their nocturnal nature. A woodrat's presence is usually only evident by the sight of its elaborate nests.

The woodrat is herbivorous, feeding on seeds, beans, nuts, and cactus pulp. Woodrats stay active all year but prepare for winter by storing seeds and fruit in their nests. In the spring, two to four tiny young are born blind and without fur, weighing only half an ounce each. At three weeks their eyes open, and by the time they are eight weeks old they are ready to go off on their own. Woodrats seldom live for more than a year because they are heavily preyed upon by almost every other animal. Their most dangerous predators include owls, hawks, snakes, coyotes, foxes, and bobcats.

Bats have hands, arms, and fingers that have been modified into thin, flexible wings, making bats the only mammals truly capable of flying. With approximately nine hundred different species, bats are the second-largest order of mammals. The Mexican, or Brazilian, free-tailed bat is a medium-size bat that measures four inches in length, weighs less than half an ounce, and has a wingspan of twelve inches. It is the only species of bat capable of moving its tail.

Despite common misconceptions, bats have good eyesight but often use their ears rather than their eyes to see. To determine where they are, bats let out a loud, high-pitched shriek above the range of human hearing and then listen for the sound to bounce back off objects in front of them. Echoes from insects, for example, give bats information about

MEXICAN FREE-TAILED BAT

the direction and distance of their prey. This method of locating objects is called echolocation.

Mexican free-tailed bats live in the desert during the warm months and then migrate south to Mexico in the fall. Bats live in colonies and usually breed in March. Approximately three months later a single baby is born. Young bats mature rapidly and are capable of flying four to six weeks after birth. Bats have few enemies, though hawks, owls, and snakes sometimes prey on them. Bats are strictly nocturnal, spending the day hanging upside down in caves, on branches, and under rocks. Although bats are found in many areas of the United States, the most famous bat habitat is in the Southwest. Carlsbad Caverns National Park in New Mexico is the home for some five million Mexican free-tailed bats. The best time to see them is in summer, when the roar of flapping wings can be heard at dusk as ten thousand bats per minute come rushing out of the caves.

Bats live all over the world except Antarctica and the Arctic. North American species are insectivorous, feeding on tiny insects that are often too small to be seen by the human eye.

The scorpion is a member of the arthropod group which includes insects, lobsters, and spiders. An arthropod is an animal whose body is made up of segments and enclosed in an outside skeleton.

Scorpions are not insects but arachnids, a class of animals that also includes spiders, ticks, and mites. Scorpions are the most primitive of all land arachnids and may have been among the first animals to leave water for land over three hundred million years ago. The most common southwestern species are the giant desert hairy scorpion, which has a black body with yellow limbs and tail, and the bark scorpion, which is mostly yellow.

Armed with a poisonous stinger at the end of its tail, the scorpion is one of the most dangerous creatures in the desert. It's bite is painful but rarely causes death to humans. The greatest danger to

SCORPION

humans comes from stepping on a scorpion or from having one crawl into clothing, beds, or sleeping bags. Some animals are able to eat scorpions because they are immune to the poison. These predators include spiders, lizards, snakes, and birds of prey. Scorpions have six pairs of limbs. The first pair has tiny pincers that are used to tear apart prey, the second has large, sharp, claws that are used as feelers and to grab prey, and the last four pairs are legs.

Unlike most other arachnids, who lay eggs, the female scorpion gives birth to live young. The newborns immediately climb onto their mother's back, where they live for one to two weeks while they are developing. Scorpions generally live alone under rocks, logs, or in burrows that they dig underground. The nocturnal scorpion is carnivorous, feeding on insects, spiders, and small mammals. Scorpions do not have teeth and eat by sucking the soft tissues and juice out of their prey. Because their mouth is small, it often takes several hours for a scorpion to consume even the smallest insect. Like many other arachnids, scorpions can go for several months or even up to a year without feeding. Some scientists believe that scorpions never drink because they get all the moisture they need from their food.

T he desert tortoise is a member of the reptile class, which also includes snakes, lizards, turtles, crocodiles, and alligators. All reptiles are ectothermic, or cold-blooded, which means they can't maintain a constant body temperature because their body heat changes with the temperature of the air. To protect itself from extreme changes in temperature, the tortoise avoids the midday heat by retreating underground and hibernates during the colder desert months. But the tortoise's most unique adaption to the desert climate is its ability to store water. The desert tortoise has its own reservoir beneath its shell. This reservoir is so big that it can hold enough water to last an entire season.

DESERT TORTOISE

In the Southwest, desert tortoises live in southwestern Utah and southern Arizona. The desert tortoise is herbivorous, feeding solely on plants like herbs, grasses, and cacti. It prefers to live in flat areas where it can easily burrow its nest below the soft ground. From May to July, the female lays two to three batches, or clutches, of eggs, each containing one to fifteen eggs. She hides the eggs at the entrance to her burrow in a shallow hole by covering them with sand. One hundred days later they hatch.

Adult tortoises can grow to be fifteen inches long, but most are less than eight inches, and all begin as two-inch hatchlings. Young tortoises have soft, leathery shells that develop into strong armor after approximately five years. But most tortoises never live to be five years old because while they are young, their soft shells make them easy targets for predators. In the past the tortoise was preyed upon by humans, who collected them for pets. The desert tortoise is now federally protected as a threatened species and it is illegal to keep a tortoise. Today its main predators are skunks, badgers, and snakes.

Tortoises are the only reptiles with a shell. The adult's shell is so thick that no predator, no matter how sharp its teeth or claws, can penetrate it. When the tortoise is in danger, it retreats inside this shell as a defense against skunks, snakes, and badgers.

Rattlesnakes smell through their long, forked tongue. When a snake's tongue comes shooting out of its mouth, it isn't preparing to sting (in fact, snakes can't sting with their tongue at all) it is actually smelling for food.

Scientists believe that snakes developed from lizards over one million years ago. Most people believe that all snakes are poisonous. While this is true of rattlesnakes, it is not true of all snakes. Western diamondbacks are the largest western rattlesnakes and can be found throughout the Southwest. They are generally three to seven feet long and make their home underground in a burrow. Mating occurs from March to May, and in the late summer four to twenty-five young are born. These baby snakes don't hatch from a shell but are born alive and measure eight to thirteen inches in length.

WESTERN DIAMONDBACK

Baby rattlesnakes are born with a small buttonlike segment on the end of their tail that is the beginning of their distinctive rattle. Made out of a material that is similar to human fingernails, a new piece is added to the rattle each time the young snake sheds its skin. These pieces fit together loosely, and when the snake shakes its tail, the interlocking segments click together to produce their famous rattling sound. Snakes shed their skin by loosening the skin around their mouth and head, then rubbing their nose on a rough surface. The snake then crawls out of the old skin, turning it inside out. This process is called molting. Rattlesnakes generally molt about three or four times a year, though this occurs less frequently as they grow older.

Snakes can't chew their food because they don't have teeth, so they simply swallow it whole. The western diamondback lives mostly on mice, rats, and rabbits. When capturing prey or when threatened, a rattlesnake will bite, releasing a poisonous venom through its sharp fangs. To avoid being bitten by a rattlesnake, don't stick your hands into a hole and be careful overturning rocks where snakes can hide. If you do get bitten by a rattlesnake, go to a hospital right away to be treated with an antivenin.

A member of the iguana family, the collared lizard is three to five inches long and is distinguished from other lizards by its bright green color and the two dark bands, or "collars," on its neck. The female undergoes an unusual color change a few days before mating, displaying bright red and orange streaks on her sides that last until she lays her eggs. She usually lays one to two clutches of eggs from June to July, each containing from one to thirteen eggs. Like most lizards, collared lizards are diurnal, though they rest during the desert's hottest afternoon hours. This rock-dwelling lizard can be found throughout the Southwest in sandy, rocky areas where it can hide in grass or shrubs.

COLLARED LIZARD

Lizards have long, brittle tails that help them to maintain their balance. These tails break quite easily so that when an enemy seizes the lizard, the lizard can break off its tail. This ability to discard all or part of the tail is known as autotomy. The tail keeps moving as though it were alive, fooling the enemy and giving the lizard time to escape. A new tail starts to grow back immediately, though it usually looks noticeably different than the original.

Survival for many reptiles depends upon the speed of their get-away. Collared lizards have been clocked going sixteen to seventeen miles an hour, ranking them among the fastest of reptiles. The collared lizard runs on all four legs until it reaches its maximum speed, at which point it will stand upright and continue running on its long hind legs. It is also able to hop and jump like a frog from rock to rock in search of food such as insects, spiders, and other small lizards.

Lizards are closely related to snakes, and like other reptiles, they are ectothermic. To compensate for its constantly changing body temperature, the lizard warms itself in the hot sun or on a warm rock, and when it gets too hot, it cools its body in the shade.

Horned lizards are easily camouflaged against the soil or rocks by their brown, gray, and black coloring. Their daggerlike head spines and sharp, projecting scales also help them blend with trees and cacti.

HORNED LIZARD

Sometimes called a horned toad, this animal is not a toad at all, but a lizard that looks like a toad. It eats like a toad by shooting out its long, sticky tongue to capture prey. The diet of the horned lizard is made up almost entirely of ants, though some species also eat other insects. There are twelve species of horned lizards in North America, and all are members of the iguana family. Horned lizards live underground and in a variety of habitats ranging from the desert floor to as high as ten thousand feet. Most are three to five inches long, and all have flat bodies, short legs, and short tails.

Like other reptiles, horned lizards are ectothermic. They use the heat of the sun to warm their body, and bury themselves in the sand to keep cool. Most horned lizards lay between twenty to thirty eggs in a deep underground tunnel. The female carefully selects the nesting site, lays her eggs, and then covers up the hole with sand. Ninety days later the eggs hatch, and within thirty minutes the newborn hatchlings are fully active and capable of fending for themselves.

Horned lizards are not fast enough to run away from their predators and are not able to break off their tail like other lizards to escape if captured. They depend first on their excellent camouflage to hide them, and then on their sharp horns and prickly scales, which make them difficult to swallow. Many animals such as hawks, snakes, and other lizards have been found dead with the horns and scales of this lizard sticking in their throats. Some species of horned lizards are capable of squirting blood from their eyes. The blood can be shot as far as four feet from one or both eyelids, and the lizards can direct the spray forward or backward. The blood stings the eyes of predators, temporarily blinding them and allowing the lizard time to get away.

Gliding gracefully on warm wind currents, the turkey vulture can most often be seen soaring over open grasslands, canyons, and foothills. With a remarkable wingspan of five feet, vultures are able to travel through the air without constantly flapping their wings. Because of this effortless flight, turkey vultures are able to fly more than one hundred miles a day. Adults have dark body feathers and bald red heads, while young vultures have black heads. The vulture's featherless head is important because it allows the bird to thrust its head into carcasses to feed without getting decaying flesh stuck in its feathers.

TURKEY VULTURE

Seen throughout the Southwest from late spring to early fall, a few birds will remain in warmer areas all winter, but most gather in flocks and migrate south. Turkey vultures do not build nests but lay their eggs in depressions on cliffs and ledges and in caves. One to three eggs are laid between February and June and are incubated for five weeks before they hatch. Turkey vulture chicks remain in the nest for nine weeks.

Adult turkey vultures average twenty-nine inches in length and weigh three pounds. They have strong eyesight, but they lack the sharp claws and sharp beak of birds of prey. They are therefore unable to catch live animals and so they live entirely on carrion, or the flesh of dead animals. Like garbage collectors, vultures get rid of waste that would otherwise decay and spread disease. In this way, the turkey vulture helps to protect other animals by keeping them free of the diseases carried by dead animals. When threatened, turkey vultures won't scratch or claw like other birds—instead they vomit. Because they live on carrion, the smell from the food they have eaten chases predators away.

Turkey vultures roost in trees and keep cool by spreading their wings to expose the largest possible surface area in order to catch a cool breeze.

Hawks are members of the raptor group, which also includes eagles and owls. The word raptor is used to describe birds of prey that have three distinct features: hooked upper beaks; feet with sharp claws, called talons; and excellent vision.

The red-tailed hawk is one of the largest and most common hawks in North America. Recognized by its broad reddish tail, a typical adult has a brown head, a light-colored chest, and a dark band of feathers on its belly. Males and females have the same coloration, but females are larger. It takes a young red-tail two years to acquire adult plumage. There are two main types of hawks: accipiters and buteos. The red-tail is a buteo, characterized by broad, blunt wings and a short tail that spreads out like a fan in flight. Accipiters have short, rounded wings and a much longer tail.

RED-TAILED HAWK

Red-tailed hawks use their long-distance vision to locate prey from high exposed perches before taking flight. Feeding on all kinds of small birds, as well as on ground squirrels, rabbits, mice, snakes, and lizards, red-tailed hawks use a direct dive to stun unsuspecting prey and sometimes eat their meal in midair. The hawk's stomach is very acidic, allowing it to devour entire birds—feathers, bones, and all. Later, the hawk will cough up a pellet containing the parts of prey it can't use or digest.

Sometimes mating for life, the red-tailed hawk builds its nest between the forked limbs of tall trees or in a cliff face. This nest will be reused year after year, unless an owl (which never builds its own nest) takes over. The female usually lays one to three eggs, which hatch after thirty days. Young red-tails remain in the nest for one to two months. Red-tailed hawks can be seen all year throughout the Southwest except above the timberline in the higher mountain areas of Colorado and Utah, where they can only be seen in the summer.

Averaging twenty-two to twenty-seven inches in length, with a wingspan of four feet or more, the raven is the largest member of the crow family. The all-black raven is often mistaken for a crow, but is nearly twice the size of its smaller cousin. Distinguished by its striking black shaggy plumage, the raven has strong feet and toes as well as a hooked beak for catching prey and tearing flesh. Although ravens live in pairs or small groups, they can often be seen roosting in numbers of up to a hundred.

Unlike desert mammals, almost all birds are diurnal and few have burrows in the ground to escape heat. Instead, birds have feathers,

RAVEN

which act as insulation. Feathers keep heat away from the skin when the weather is hot and keep out the cold in the winter. The raven is omnivorous, feeding on almost anything from large insects to fruit to small birds and mammals. Like the turkey vulture the raven is a scavenger, and its favorite foods include carrion. Sometimes it will bury excess food in the ground, though it rarely ever returns to retrieve its cache.

The raven is an aerial acrobat. It will sometimes challenge an eagle or a hawk that enters its territory, and it soars, tumbles, and rolls through the air in its mating displays. Ravens mate in the air and then nest in rocky cliffs or in tall trees. The female lays three to six spotted eggs in February or March, which hatch after an eighteen-day incubation period. After the babies, called nestlings, hatch, the female swallows the eggshells to clean out the nest. Cared for by both parents, the young raven will stay in its nest for five to six weeks.

The raven has adapted to the most rugged desert habitats and can be found in all areas of the Southwest.

The roadrunner lives year round in the Southwest and is a special favorite in New Mexico, where it was declared the state bird in 1949.

R oadrunners are swift, ground-dwelling birds that live in all areas of the Southwest. They have been found at elevations as high as five thousand feet and as low as sea level, though the most likely place to find them is in open, flat areas where cacti grow. The roadrunner's main food is grasshoppers, but it also eats insects, crickets, lizards, and small snakes. After the roadrunner catches its prey, it beats the animal against a rock until it dies and then swallows the food whole.

ROADRUNNER

Although roadrunners can fly, they spend most of their time on the ground. The roadrunner runs with its head and tail stretched out. When it wants to stop, it simply raises its tail and comes to an abrupt halt. This bird got its name from its habit of racing down roads in front of moving vehicles and then darting to safety in the brush. Two feet in length, half of which is tail, the roadrunner has long, sturdy legs and a pointed bill. Distinguished by its bushy crown of raised feathers, it has a brown upper body that is streaked with black and green and spotted with white flecks. Its neck is white or pale brown, and it has a white belly. When excited, the roadrunner will raise its crest revealing a patch of white skin behind the eye that is half pale blue and half bright red.

Roadrunners are members of the cuckoo family, a species of bird known for placing its eggs in the nests of other birds, tricking them into raising the cuckoo's young. Roadrunners, however, raise their own young. They build their nests out of twigs in low trees or cacti. The female lays two to six eggs that hatch after eighteen days. While the eggs are developing, the male incubates them. One to three weeks after birth, the young roadrunner can catch its own food and is ready to be fully independent.

The gila woodpecker is the most common woodpecker in the desert Southwest. Seen year round, its body is covered with a distinctive black-and-white striped feather pattern, and the male has a bright red cap on the top of its head. A medium-size woodpecker, this species is nine inches long and makes its home in and around giant cacti. Gila woodpeckers can be easily located by listening for the loud knocking sound they make drilling holes in trees or cacti or the voice they use to call other woodpeckers, which sounds like a sharp, repetitive laugh.

Woodpeckers have strong feet with two toes facing forward and two facing back, while most other birds have three toes forward and one back. This unique adaptation, along

GILA WOODPECKER

with a strong tail, helps keep the woodpecker balanced as it rests against tree trunks and cacti. Woodpeckers spend most of their time hacking away at dead or rotten plants in search of burrowing bugs. Although their main diet is insects, gila woodpeckers also eat cactus fruits, bird eggs, small birds, and lizards.

The gila woodpecker drills a hole in a large cactus approximately one foot deep and lays three to four pure white eggs in this nest. Both parents take turns incubating the eggs for two weeks until it is time for them to hatch. The young are featherless and blind at birth and are cared for by both parents for about a year.

Gila woodpeckers have long, chisel-like bills that they use to drill holes in trees, houses, telephone poles, and cacti. Their strong head muscles protect the woodpecker from the constant hammering, and their long sticky tongue pulls insects from these holes.

Young Gambel's quails are streaked with downy feathers and have a miniature topknot on their head to match their parents'.

The striking Gambel's quail is common in the dry desert habitats of the Southwest. Although the Gambel's quail is often mistaken for the California quail, the distinction between the two birds can be easily made by looking at their bellies and sides. The California quail has a scalelike feather pattern on its belly and brown sides streaked with white. The Gambel's quail has an unscaled belly pattern, and its sides are chestnut streaked with white. Both sexes of the Gambel's and the California quail have a distinc-

GAMBEL'S QUAIL

tive teardrop topknot on the top of their head that distinguishes them from other quails. The male Gambel's is identified by a black neck and black belly patch; female and young Gambel's are grayish all over.

There are over one hundred species of quail in the world, seven of which can be found in the United States. Quails are gregarious birds that live in large groups called coveys. In cooler southwestern climates, five to six families will flock together to endure the cold winter. Mating occurs from early April to late May, and the cock's call can be heard throughout the breeding area. The cock (male) displays himself to the hen (female), bowing and dancing around her as he chatters mating sounds. Later, the hen lays twelve to sixteen cream-colored spotted eggs in a hidden nest lined with grass. The chicks are active immediately after birth but cannot fly for a week to ten days. Cared for by both parents, the young quails are independent after four weeks.

The Gambel's quail feeds on seeds, insects, and small lizards. Reluctant to fly, the quail remains close to the ground, avoiding tall vegetation where it may not see an approaching hawk or raven.

One of the most familiar songs in the desert is the rapid monotone call of the cactus wren. A member of the songbird family, the cactus wren is the largest wren in the United States. Cactus wrens have a brown body streaked with white, a black-spotted white breast, and a long, curved bill that is almost as long as their entire head. Although they are considered large in comparison to other wrens, they are still small in terms of other animals that inhabit the desert. Cactus wrens have many predators, but the animals that prey upon them most heavily are cats, snakes, hawks, and roadrunners.

CACTUS WREN

Cactus wren nests are easy to find because they are almost twelve inches long and shaped like a football. Built from grass, stems, and twigs, the nests are lined with soft feathers and built between the dried branches of cacti. In populated areas, the cactus wren is resourceful enough to use whatever materials are available, such as newspaper, string, rope, cotton, and rags. The male builds several nests close together to attract a potential mate. The female will then select the best constructed and most hidden nest to lay her eggs. The unused nests then serve as winter roosting places or as decoys to lead enemies away from the real nest. The female lays two clutches of eggs, each contains three to six pink-spotted eggs. The female incubates the eggs by herself while the male brings her food. After sixteen days the eggs begin to hatch, and the young remain in the nest for about three weeks.

These birds are insectivorous, searching the ground for insects, seeds, and small bugs. Because there is little or no water in the desert, cactus wrens take dust baths to keep clean. Squatting on the ground, the bird spreads its wings and ruffles its body around in the dirt so the dust can penetrate the feathers to remove trapped material.

A familiar sight throughout the Southwest, especially in lower elevations, the cactus wren was declared the state bird of Arizona in 1931.

Adult mourning doves take turns incubating their eggs. They protect the eggs from overheating by keeping them cool with their own bodies. Male doves have a lower body temperature than do females so males sit on the eggs during the day and females take their turn at night.

A member of the pigeon family, the mourning dove is the most common dove in the Southwest. Twelve inches long with a long, pointed tail, the mourning dove has a brownish coloring that is accented by a pinkish belly and black-spotted wings. Two other similar doves, the inca and the white-winged, are also resident in the Southwest, but both are smaller and resemble miniature mourning doves. A mourning dove can be discovered by listening carefully at dusk or dawn for the sad, mournful call for which this bird is named.

MOURNING DOVE

Like all pigeons, the mourning dove builds a very poor nest. Gathering a few sticks and some grass, it usually nests in low trees or cacti but will nest on the ground if it can't find covering elsewhere. When attempting to mate, the male parades around the female, arching his back and bowing his head up and down repeatedly to attract her. Once he is successful, two eggs are laid that hatch after fifteen to twenty days. While adults eat weeds, seeds, and insects, young doves are fed regurgitated food from their parents' beaks. Young doves are also fed "crop milk" which is produced in a sack at the back of the female's throat. Doves and pigeons are the only birds capable of producing this "milk" for their young. After two short weeks, the young doves are ready to leave the nest.

Mourning doves have an effective distraction tactic used to defend the nest. If threatened, the adult flutters or falls to the ground and flops around pretending to be injured. This way the predator is more interested in the injured bird than in the eggs or the young doves. Once the adult has led the enemy astray, it can fly safely away and return to the nest. Mourning doves are persistently hunted in the wild by both animals and humans, who kill this bird for sport. Mourning doves are also hunted by cats, dogs, and birds of prey.

GLOSSARY

accipiter: A bird-eating forest hawk with short wings and a long tail.

antivenin: A serum that contains antibodies to counteract the poisonous venom transmitted by snakes and other reptiles.

arthropod: An animal whose body is made up of segments and enclosed in an outside skeleton. Arthropods include insects, lobsters, and spiders.

autotomy: A reflex separation of a part or a limb from the body.

burrow: A hole in the ground made by an animal for shelter and a home.

buteo: A soaring hawk with long, rounded wings and a short tail.

cache: A hiding place especially for storing food or provisions.

camouflage: Color and patterns that help an animal blend into its surroundings.

carnivorous: Eating mainly meat.

class: A group of animals that are alike in some way.

clutch: A nest of eggs or a group of chicks.

covey: A small flock of birds.

diurnal: Active in the daytime.

echolocation: A process for locating distant or invisible objects by means of reflecting sound waves.

ectothermic: An animal having a body temperature that is not internally regulated but affected by its environment; cold-blooded.

endangered species: A group of animals threatened with extinction.

estivation: The summer resting period.

extinct: No longer existing.

gestation: The period of growth before birth during which the unborn young develop within the mother's body.

habitat: The place where an animal lives and grows.

herbivorous: Feeding mainly on plants.

hibernation: A period of rest or inactivity, usually in winter, in which activity stops and the body processes slow down.

incubate: To sit on eggs to warm them so they hatch.

insectivorous: Feeding mainly on insects.

mammal: A class of warm-blooded animals covered with hair; they give birth to live young and feed them with milk from mammary glands. Hair can be fur, wool, quills, and even certain horns.

migrate: To move from one place to another for food or to breed.

molt: To shed an outer layer of skin, hair, feathers, shell, or horns.

nocturnal: Active at night.

omnivorous: Feeding on both plants and animals.

predator: An animal that catches and devours another animal.

protected species: A group of animals protected by state or federal law because they are either endangered or threatened.

raptor: A bird of prey with a hooked beak, sharp talons, and excellent vision. Includes owls, hawks, and eagles.

reptile: An ectothermic animal with scales that moves on its belly or on short, small legs. Includes lizards, snakes, turtles, alligators, and crocodiles.

species: A biological group of animals that breed with one another and share the same general physical characteristics.

talons: The sharp claws of an animal, especially those of a bird of prey.

threatened species: A group of animals whose numbers are decreasing, bringing the group close to endangerment.

venom: A poison transmitted to prey by biting or stinging.